Christmas [illegible] e Is Golden

By

Darren Paddon

MAPLE
PUBLISHERS

Christmas Time Is Golden

Author: Darren Paddon

First Published in 2024

ISBN 978-1-83538-338-4 (Paperback)
978-1-83538-339-1 (E-Book)

Book Cover Design, Illustration and Book Layout by:
White Magic Studios
www.whitemagicstudios.co.uk

Published by:
Maple Publishers
Fairbourne Drive, Atterbury,
Milton Keynes,
MK10 9RG, UK
www.maplepublishers.com

A CIP catalogue record for this title is available from the British Library.

A loser?

It all seems like a dream now but in my deepest heart I feel it like a ghost haunting me everywhere. I never believed in time travels. I can say with all my faith I don't.

Christmas was always a happy time for me, that all changed. Readers of this should never play with time. You never know when time can rearrange itself.

As a young boy I always had a very special bond with my grandparents. And as I write about my memories I feel an emptiness that can never be filled. The house my Grandparents lived in had a very homely warm presence that called out to me, 'you're loved, and always wanted.' They made Christmas a magical time. I love the Christmas stories. My Nan would tell them with so much excitement and passion in her voice.

It transported me there in my mind like a bus pass with no restrictions or time limits, for free. A story that really tickled my pickle was always the nativity story from the good book, a little Christmas Bible. The story had it all – murder, evil kings, angels, Christmas stars and faithful animals and gifts.

As the years went speeding on so fast like a joy ride in a stolen car being chased by the police, adulthood was in front of me. Age is a race that no one can win, young and old; it beats us all like a number one in the charts. And I was no different. I have loved, lost, cried but mostly lost.

I am very ashamed of my achievements; the lovers in my life, they have all seen me for the loser and boozer that I am. They all have found happiness away from me, maybe I am cursed. I am swimming in a sea of self-pity. I find myself now living all alone - fat, looking forward to eating my feelings away day after day, wishing for me to pass away, saying to myself - welcome to forty.

It's morning again, I mumbled to myself as I opened my eyes. Not just any morning but Monday. I don't know why I hate Mondays, I had no job and nowhere to go, but silly, I thought to myself. I started getting dressed; no wash, no brushing of teeth and didn't give a monkey's. I had no pride left in me, the hunger called me from inside my fat belly, 'feed me now.' With no food in my cupboard, empty, I felt like the Doggy in the nursery rhyme: 'no bone for me' as I laughed to myself.

I had a wonderful idea. Time to go to the pub for a full English breakfast, like a bird of prey looking for its victim. But for me my victim at this time is a large fry and cold Fosters. I left for my journey in my wheelchair that I have to use now because of an illness three years ago. Feeling like a spaceman in the chair, with a fake smile on my face and the sun beaming down on me like a spot light. Thank goodness the wheel chair is electric because if I had to use my arms in this prickly heat I would melt like lard. It could have been all psychological, I think I smell like bacon when hot and perspiring, wishing I had a wash.

I see the pub in the distance like an old friend inviting me in, offering me shade. When you're obese, sun is not your friend. Like a vampire I stay away a bit like the opposite sex stay away

from me like I have leprosy. Females seem to think that being in a wheelchair like a deadly disease.

I roll into the Parchmaers Pub as the smell of beer and cheap perfume pollutes the air. The pub is as always the same with same men and the song that always comes to my mind, the 'Piano man' by Billy Joel. There is an old man sitting next to me making love to his tonic & gin. I went to the same table fifteen. I really don't like any changes. In my mind it's my table; like the pub it's my friend. It's madness, inside I'm screaming, IT'S MADNESS!!!

Once I knew my table was reserved for me only, I knew my table's virginity was safe, I went to the bar. It was sweet to hear, "Can I take your order?" The Lady that was serving me was beautiful, blond hair, blue eyes. She looked like Aphrodite herself. Really wishing that I had treated myself to a shower this morning, I answered nervously, "A large breakfast and a pint of Fosters." "Table number?" "Fifteen," I replied. "Would you like me to carry your drink to your table for you?" "Yes, please," I replied emphatically.

I slowly went to my table and waited for my food like a rabid dog. When you're greedy and on the large side, minutes will seem like hours. Panic over, I didn't care who served my plate - it could have been the king himself. All I was thinking was, 'get it in my belly and don't spare the horses.' Did I eat it all? Yes I did, it's not my doing, it's my bad, bad belly, who I blame; and words I have repeated to myself a thousand times: I will start my diet tomorrow, but tomorrow is always a day away. And I giggled to myself - I better head home and listen to more silence.

As here outside the window was a circus on the green opposite the pub. Where did this circus appear from? Am I seeing things, where did the customers vanish? "Hello," I called out. The building was empty like my love life. I sped to the exit, knocking my table flying. I am out, the carnival was still there. Am I dreaming? Was I high on the cheap perfume or a stroke or crazy? Or did I choke on my breakfast and died? Jeepers creepers, what a morning! I grabbed my phone and tried to dial for help. No network. Where or when? Was it the first person I saw coming out of the large tent or am I just crackers?

A little red-haired white-faced clown, all the colours that you couldn't have ever imagined, like a rainbow. It was so bright everywhere, really beautiful! For a moment, I forgot how scared I was, I nearly soiled myself but luckily it was just anus moisture like an orange that has been juiced until empty, similar to my prospects in my life achievements. The Clown gave me a creepy smile and started to walk very quickly over to me. I screamed out in fear jumping like a jelly fish, "Don't hurt me, please. Be gentle, sir." I had my man bag ready to strike the clown thinking if only I had a rape alarm. I just had my wallet, phone keys. The clown was right in my face laughing at me, "I'm Johnny the Clown. I'm from a time long ago, from a star called Earendel 12.9 billion years ago, and I'm here to help you. My divine **Kali, Goddess of time** likes you and wants to give you a very special gift."

Kali, Goddess of time

"Am I dreaming?" The jester replied, "Dreaming." Laughing loudly, he pulled a very old looking paper out of his front pocket, reading, "Your name is Fred Mike Smith." "Yes," I replied softly.

Still laughing like a lunatic the clown was, I was thinking to myself, this has got to be a prank. "Boulder-Dash," I shouted, "I WILL WAKE UP SOON!", thinking I need a clean trousers badly. **"Kali** really needs to have little chat and life review with you before you receive a very special time trident," the clown clapped his hands and spoke the words. "Time is the divine light." Give me flight, I started to hover. "Did **Isaac Newton** have **gravity** all wrong in one late summer of **1666?"** I said at the top of my voice as I kept rising up as easy as a feather dances in the wind. The wheelchair left on the ground below like a ton weight. I was looking for Johnny the clown, nowhere to be seen up in the cosmos. Flying like an angel, I was seeing stars and planets, passing by them with no restrictions or limits.

I always wanted to go to space. Loved Star wars film before puberty came knocking on my biological body's door like a burglar stealing innocence, and may I say – excitement? In the distance a ball of light, I was speeding for the light thinking I'm going to crash right in to the beacon of light. Then I will wake up and request a brain scan immediately!!! Also give alcohol a miss. No crash at all, I was into the attractive white light like a moth to the flame. Now I knew how Samson felt in the Bible

being under Delilah's magnetic beauty in the **Biblical book of Judges chapters 13-16.** Then all at once I landed on my feet standing unaided for the first time in years - a miracle! Or am I just in a very deep sleep using **Delta waves 0.5 and 4HZ** range brain waves?

As I looked around exploring with my eyes, I saw a golden house with diamond doors down a long red path. The sky was so blue it looked like I was in paradise - beautiful plants and trees with red apples and strawberries, and red & white roses growing everywhere, as far as my eyes could see. Still all alone I started walking to the golden house, walking down that red path. It wasn't brick, I couldn't believe my eyes- red ruby! The path seemed to go on and on, I kept marching on like there was an invisible force pushing me to the golden doors. I made it. I was frightened but I was too curious for my own good, they say that's what killed the cat in the end. I just hope they've got that proverb wrong.

On the doors was written **domumom or casa quid off angeli** that looked like Latin. I recognised 'angel', what a dream! I shouted out loud in a very high pitched voice. I began to knock, knock, knock three times using the door knocker that looked like a large round clock with a silver ring in the middle of the clock face. The double doors started to open like magic so I took a step through the entrance. I thought, no I was so wrong, it was just a river bank. I'm not going to swim across with my poo bruised trousers, surely sink like gold, don't want to drown. Just then on the water a little wooden boat was rowing towards me. The man rowing the boat was wearing a black cloak. Right away I noticed a necklace around the very dark figure's neck. It looked like a blue moon. The boat was very close to the river bank. I wanted to run but my feet would not move a muscle.

Glued to the spot I was helpless, trying to fight back my tears. The boat docked. Now I could see him more clearly. **OH MY GOD A SKELETON!** What started out being a fun dream is turning into a horrible nightmare. The skeleton started speaking to me. "My name is **Charon.** I've been given a job to row you to the other side to the Goddess of time who goes by so many names. I call her **Horae.** Come aboard, I got a busy job delivering. **Psyche** never resting. Only receiving half a silver coin each boat journey." I come aboard, I had no free will, like I was a puppet on a string under my master's motions and movements. "Please be seated," the dark cloaked figure demanded.

Gliding Across

I sat down on the damp wooden seat, then the boat started moving across the river. Trying to ask the boat man, where am I? I could not make a sound. The water wave gliding across was now red like fire hands reaching from the river of fire for the boat to come aboard but never reaching the vessel. Loud barking killed the sound of silence. The hooded man spoke, "Don't worry that's only ***Cerberus,*** *you're quite safe." The boat was slowing then came to a complete stop. "Your trip on the boat has come to an end. Follow the green path of righteousness to the gates of* ***Paradisus."***
I quickly exited the boat. Like magic, I found myself standing on the river bank on my own. Again the water was blue, again back to paradise.

I see a green path. I start stepping, more like ice skating, not on ice, but beautiful green emerald, pulled along by an invisible energy towards the giant golden gates that started to open as I skated towards them like a bullet being fired out of a gun. Then I stopped dead before entering. A man came out, saying to me in a lovely welcoming voice, "My name is **Saint Peter** and you're here to claim a gift." I replied, "You know more than me, sir, can I ask a question? AM I DEAD!!! ?" Peter replied, "It will all be clear to you very soon."

A dog came running out with his tail wagging. Peter started laughing, saying, "I'm sorry we couldn't stop **Clyde.** He got very excited and wanted to see you!" Clyde, my special dog, the best

friend a boy ever had. Jumping up, licking my face like when Clyde was a puppy. Not gone, not deceased, but living a full happy life. With tear filled eyes I kissed my late dog's head. I whispered to him, "Good boy, love you." Peter said, "I will just take Clyde back because he likes to try a run away some times. **100 times so far since** he's been staying with us! Wait right where you are." I saw Clyde walking with Peter back through the large gates and into the mist.

I waited patiently then I heard a voice out of the mist calling my name - Fred Mike Smith. I replied, "Hello." Walking towards me was a beautiful lady in a white dress, blue eyes, blond shiny long hair, red lips like cherry brandy, the scent of roses surrounding her as she walked and stood beside me and spoke. "My name's Kali. Well, that's one of my names. I can control time. I've been watching you from afar and I need to give you gift for a short time but we need to do a life review!" "Can't I just go home?" I asked nervously. The beautiful **Kali** replied softly, "You're the first mortal I've picked for this wonderful opportunity to travel through space and time. Do the life review with me and if you really want go after the assessment that can be done. So note it, hold on to my hand." So I did.

Call out 'Tempus'

A flash of light, and we appeared in a white room with a glass table in the middle of the room with two white chairs next to each other. "Let's begin, please sit. Look directly into the table's eye." I was trying to control the need to look at Kali, Beauty. In the glass eye I saw myself as a young boy of nine in my old class. Mrs. Green's math lesson and on my school desk a work sheet in front of me. Lots of sums. List of sums went on. **Sample 9x6=54, 8x3=24, 16x10=160,** they went on. Mrs. Green went round the class asking what answers we have put down. I was the first pupil she came to. I gave the teacher three right answers, the other pupils started calling me names – teacher's pet, the wise owl, Mr. know-it-all. I put the wrong answers after that and kept playing stupid to fit in for years. **Kali** paused the review to ask me, "Why did you not shine when you could?" "I don't know," I replied.

Kali says in her angel soft voice, "Let's move on to your love life. Look there." I was a young man in the twenties lying next to the only woman that I ever loved. Her beautiful blond hair. It was **Carol Clark.** Feeling the love I still carried in my heart and soul for Miss C. Clark, it could never end. I could see all the hurtful words, making her feel unloved, needing so much to be the Man. I started out to be wanting to be her rock but ended up being a horrid shock.

Kali paused the review. **Kali** starts saying in a soft voice, "What if you could change your past only in your life time?" I answered, "Of course." Kali says one word, **tempus.** All at once, she's holding a large golden fork with a blue rock in the pole at the top. Kali starts to demonstrate how this object works. "Call out 'tempus'." It will appear when called. Keep a life event in your head, it will temporarily send you back but you will only know the results when you're in your present time. When you leap through time, any interference with your life choices, the consequences could change the universe forever." Before I could ask for more information **Kali** vanished.

I was all alone in that white room, still very bewildered and very emotional, and more importantly, terrified!!! As looked around the room I noticed - no ceiling just endless stars, astronomer's wet dreams. Remembering **Kali's** instructions I spoke the word 'tempus'. A flash of white bright light all around, then in my hand appeared the beautiful shimmering gold time trident. In my mind I kept thinking of the Mrs. Green's math paper. I was in the cosmos again for just a second. I was in the past doing the math paper. I put the sum right, I wanted to say 'hello' to my kind old teacher. But before I had time to speak I felt a static charge through my body. I was in the cosmos for a second, then I was back in that lovely review room once more.

My mind returned to my first love. I was thinking how I drove **Carol Clark** away into the arms of my former friend, **Tom Gugins.** My memory strayed to how **Judas** betrayed **Jesus** in the Gospel **of Matthew 26:15,** but **Tom betrayed** me for a lot less than thirty pieces of silver.

I called out 'tempus' once more. The trident appeared in my hand. In my mind thinking of the past, I met Tom. In a flash I was in the cosmos. Then I was back in the past at **Southdowns College.** It was Tom's first day in the IT, Room 205. My lecturer **Dianna Scott** wanted Tom to shadow me for the day. I waited for her to ask me that question, and she did!! I could remember that's how we became friends. Not this time around, I was thinking. I shouted, "NOT ON YOUR NELLY, GOOD DAY TO YOU!!!" A static charge again, I was in space, then in a flash, back in the white room. I was thinking I needed to put right what once went wrong with **Carol** and me.

On my calling out **tempus** the gold trident appeared in my hand like magic. In my mind I had the memory the first kiss between us. In a flash I was flying in space like **Superman** like a speeding rocket then bang! I was back, about to kiss my **Carol** then I softly whispered, "Always remember one thing, how special you are and your lips are the only lips I want to touch mine, and love you." Before she could reply I was in the cosmos. I was back in the white room. My heart was breaking. I wanted to stay with **Carol Clark** in that time line. I started to cheer myself up and the Christmases I had growing up.

I did not say tempus!

Something went wrong, I did not say **tempus!** I'm back in the past Christmas day having turkey dinner at the able with my late Nan & Grandad. The decorated Christmas tree, old familiar feeling of being wanted and appreciated. I finished my dinner. Then a flash, it was the same day and dinner again, I was full like a balls bum!! I said to dear Nan, "I'm not hungry." Her face looked hurt. I was repeating the same Christmas dinner over and over. Each meal looked like the food was decaying, the smell was putrid. Trying not to be sick at the table I vomited.

I will never forget my Nan crying thinking it was her cooking. They could not see the day aging at all, only I could. When was it all going to end, I kept saying 'tempus'!! OVER AND OVER. Then it all went dark I screamed NAN, GRANDAD!!! It was complete silence. A white light everywhere. It was so bright I closed my eyes. I heard **Kali's** voice. I opened my eyes. I was in a hospital bed hooked up to heart monitor, machines all beeping away, the beautiful angel was now a Doctor.

In a very soft kind voice she said very slowly, "Don't try talking." I couldn't anyway if I wanted to. I had an oxygen mask over my face. "I'm **Doctor Karlie.** You have had **anaphylaxis reaction** caused by bee **venom.** Your heart went into **cardiac arrest.** Your heart stopped beating for three minutes." She took my hand and whispered, "Everything will be ok," and smiled at me. "There's a young blond lady in the hospital waiting room to see you. Shall I say, up for visitors?" She gave me a wink as she left the room.

Lying there trying to make sense of it all. **Carol Clark** came running in. She spoke these words, "I will love you always and can't lose you again, Fred!" I pulled off the mask and mumbled in a weak voice, "Love you too! Always! **Carol,** will you marry me?" She answered, "Yes!" putting her arms around me. It's true, love can last until the end of time and beyond!!

Time is a very precious gift, don't waste it.

www.ingramcontent.com/pod-product-compliance
Ingram Content Group UK Ltd.
Pitfield, Milton Keynes, MK11 3LW, UK
UKHW051108161224
452405UK00002B/8